MORE MYSTERY BY KRISTINE KATHRYN RUSCH

THE SMOKEY DALTON SERIES

ALSO BY KRISTINE KATHRYN RUSCH

THE FEY SERIES

THE ORIGINAL BOOKS OF THE FEY

The Sacrifice: Book One of the Fey

The Changeling: Book Two of the Fey

The Rival: Book Three of the Fey

The Resistance: Book Four of the Fey

Victory: Book Five of the Fey

THE BLACK THRONE

The Black Queen: Book One of the Black Throne

The Black King: Book Two of the Black Throne

THE QAVNERIAN PROTECTORATE

The Reflection on Mount Vitaki: Prequel to the Qavnerian Protectorate

The Kirilli Matter: The First Book of the Qavnerian Protectorate

Barkson's Journey: The Second Book of the Qavnerian Protectorate

Incident at Serebro Academy: The Third Book of the Qavnerian Protectorate

DEATH DAY

A RUSCH CRIME STORY

KRISTINE KATHRYN RUSCH

WMG
PUBLISHING

DEATH DAY

DEATH DAY

At 11:45 p.m. on July 30, Sabrina Greenwald sat in a hotel suite in the most unlikely place for her to be: The Strip, Las Vegas, Nevada. The hotel suite cost almost $10,000 per night (and that was a discounted rate because it was summer), but she figured why the hell not.

Every single measure she had—and she had dozens of them—said that she would die on July 31.

She had known this since she started casting at the age of eight.

Precocious, her mother had said proudly.

Time-limited, her grandmother would reply. *The powers come early to those who will die young.*

Her mother and grandmother could cast too. They all

1

had the powers of premonition, and those powers were not blessed ones.

In fact, her grandmother, a dyspeptic woman who never saw the good in anything, gave birth to a daughter and cried. Then she promptly named that daughter Pandora, as a reminder of all the bad things that were escaping into the world.

That daughter, Sabrina's mother, said the name Pandora was a beacon of hope, because no matter what evil got unleashed, hope would always remain.

You're dreamin', girl, Grandmama would say every single time they had that conversation. Every. Single. Time.

Sabrina was a mix of both—optimistic on her good days and pessimistic on her bad ones.

This was a bad one, and she had promised herself it would be a good one. Her last day on Earth should have been filled with celebration—good meals, friends, lots of love.

In fact, her mother suggested it at Christmas.

The best part? her mother had said. *We'll all be there with you, so whatever comes, we can mitigate it.*

Sabrina had shaken her head. *Or something bad could happen to you, too.*

Nothing bad will happen to Mama, Sabrina's twin brother, Darren, had said. *I would make sure of that.*

As if he could. He never believed that Sabrina would die. They were together forever, he would say, and she would give him a small smile. They weren't going to be together forever, and she saw it as her duty to make sure he was prepared for that.

Like most males in the family, Darren had no precog abilities. He tried not to dismiss them, especially since he benefited from them, but he didn't want to believe either.

I like to think we have free will, he would say, and everyone would nod.

Only Grandmama would confront him. *Free will and knowing the future ain't mutually exclusive, son*, she would say. *There's folks who can overcome what's predicted.*

But Sabrina was convinced her grandmother really didn't believe that. Sabrina figured her grandmother would say that as a sop to non-believers.

She had this hunch because, when she was thirteen, she overheard her grandmother and her mother talking.

The big ones, we can't wish those away, Grandmama said. *They're touchstones in our lives—birth, death. You know this, Pandy. Those are fixed points. And there ain't nothing we can do about Sabrina's short life, except love her to pieces now.*

Fixed points. The birth could be predicted. The death could be predicted. Everything in between—unless you were one of those "important" people whose lives seemed to be in constant flux—was subject to the vagaries of fate. Or, as Darren would say, free will.

Darren had talked to Sabrina a lot during this past year. He was always encouraging her to fight her future.

He wanted her to stay with him, pretend that the date wasn't coming up. *His* death date—predicted at his birth as was the family tradition—wouldn't come for another sixty-five years. Her brother would live a long life.

He kept saying to her that if she believed the predictions to be true, then he had nothing to fear by being at her side.

There's a lot worse things than dying, Darren, she would say to him. He finally made her list them, so she did: *Disfigurement, dismemberment, and traumatic brain injury resulting in dementia. I'm afraid, Darre, that you might become a vegetable just by staying at my side. Think about it: your death date doesn't say you'll live a* good *life. Just that you'll live a long one.*

He had shrugged it off, like the young male he was. Immortal, invincible, ready to take on the world.

She had never felt that way. She had always known she was not going to have a lot of chances.

In the end, she fled her home in the middle of the night, more than a week ago now. She took comfort in the fact that her family wasn't tech-savvy enough to track her via her bank accounts or her credit card usage.

And she knew them well enough to know that if she didn't return, if she disappeared off the face of the earth (which was a distinct possibility), then they would try to use their magic to track her, which had never worked, not even when she was a toddler. Something about her magic made her impervious to theirs.

Then, and only then, would they hire someone without

magic, someone who would use modern techniques to find her.

Tracking her to this hotel wouldn't be hard for someone like that.

Her family, though, would have a great deal of difficulty with it.

Which was why she couldn't call Darren right now. She might blunder and tell him she was in Las Vegas, a city her entire family hated. They always said it had fake luck and harmed people, but now that she was here, she wondered if that was true.

It was just a place, after all. A very interesting and exclusive place, but still, just a place—even if it was the nicest place she had stayed in her entire life.

Although she could do without the gold décor in the second master suite, and the gold trim throughout the other six rooms.

Yes, if she called Darren, she would let something like that slip. And then she would laugh, and he would remember it. Darren was good at remembering every little detail.

She missed him. She couldn't remember the last time she had voluntarily separated herself from him.

The fact that she had survived to this very moment buoyed her, just a little. It was already July 31 in East Cape, New Zealand, and had been for about ten hours now.

So, ten hours of July 31 had gone by somewhere in the world, and she was still alive.

She had no idea how these death dates really worked. Was she scheduled to die at a particular date and time, and was that time fixed to a time zone?

Or was she set to die on the date and the date only?

The fact that she was still here after ten hours probably meant her death was affixed to a time.

And if that was the case, then maybe it was affixed to a place.

And if that was true, why had no one told her? *Hey, Sabrina, avoid Kalamazoo, Michigan. If you go there at 4 p.m. on July 31, you'll die.*

Easy-peasy. But the way her family conjured, they seemed to only get the date, and nothing more.

And everyone she consulted seemed confused by the nuance. They all believed the death date was a death date.

It infuriated her so much that she actually thought of going to New Zealand, just to shake her fist at her death day and tell the universe to bring it on.

But she respected fate. And she worried that shaking her fist at her death day might actually force her into some risky situations that she wouldn't normally be in.

Like being in a hotel suite on The Strip in Las Vegas— or so her brother might say. Or her pessimistic grandmother.

Still, going to New Zealand felt wrong, just like fleeing to American Samoa felt wrong too. If she was going to die on July 31, she wasn't the kind of person to wring the very last second out of the day.

6

Besides, she thought it might end up as one of those cosmic jokes: She could see herself beginning a celebration on what she thought was 12:01 a.m. in American Samoa, only to discover that her watch or some clock was off, and she had three minutes left in the day.

And then, for some reason, in some way, she would die.

So better to go somewhere new and different, where her family couldn't become collateral damage. She had given this years of thought and had come up with the plan she was living now.

She was using what was left of the inheritance she had gotten from her father to splurge in Las Vegas. The splurge had sounded like a fun idea to her twenty-something self, which was when she put the money away.

Later—as she thought about booking this, so a long time later—she realized that renting an expensive suite in a part of the country used to great wealth was an even better idea than she had originally thought.

This damn place was more secure than a bank vault. Getting into this room took special keys, lots of codes, and most important of all, money.

Not even someone with an invitation could get in easily.

If she never left the room, she was about as safe as a person could be without a trusted bodyguard.

The suite was gorgeous, even with the gold, maybe the nicest place she had ever stayed. It was technically called a villa by the hotel, and the villa level wasn't even the best the hotel had to offer. That would have been the palace level, but that level only came in three- and four-bedrooms, and she felt like that was overkill, no pun intended.

This was overkill, too. A two-bedroom suite on the top floor of the exclusive wing of the hotel, with an exclusive gated entrance and a private lobby, for heaven's sake. Just to get on the elevator required a key card *and* a special code. To get past the private lobby required the key card and a different code.

Then there was the gated entrance, guarded by the butler, who stood at his station doing God knows what, because she had no use for him. She had actually asked him if he could take time off, because she didn't need him, and he politely said, *No ma'am, I'm here in case you need me.*

He sounded very firm about that, so she didn't argue. Besides, he couldn't get past the gated entrance either without his key card and a code special to him. So, if he tried something untoward, the hotel would have a record of it.

She didn't believe they would hire anyone in his position who would do something untoward. There were companies that vetted people for that, and she was certain the hotel would use those companies.

The suite was, then, in some ways, a bunker. It was effectively impenetrable to anyone who did not belong.

But it didn't feel like a bunker. It was—according to the hotel's advertising—3,300 square feet, bigger than her house back home. Her house also lacked a butler's pantry, although her house (at least) had a full kitchen.

This place did not. The expectation was probably that if someone wanted a full meal, they could either go to one of the 100 restaurants in the hotel complex or bring in a celebrity chef (for an extra fee) who would probably bring food from his own kitchen.

The suite had even more than that, though. A real fireplace in the den, and a private seating area that could be closed off from the elements. Then there were the bedrooms, one with a king-sized bed that was bigger than any king-sized bed she had ever seen. The bathroom was so spacious, her entire kitchen could have fit into it, and it had some amenities that she had never seen before. She thought she might look them up, but she was lazy.

What was the point of learning something new when she literally would not be around to use that knowledge?

In fact, that feeling had slowed her down all day. It was the ultimate *What's the point?* She understood the point of wills and planning for the days when she wasn't going to be around anymore.

She understood the point of planning for her death, taking it—whatever it would be—away from her family. She had even done all the due diligence ahead of time, seeing a slew of actual doctors to find out if she had some kind of ticking time bomb inside her body, something like an aneurysm that would just erupt and kill her.

She was startled to learn that some things, like a blood

vessel in the brain set to burst, weren't always visible on modern tests, which made her wonder aloud to the sixth doctor what the point of testing was at all. He had said, in that blunt way some doctors had, that in her case, she had gone long past the point of testing.

There was nothing wrong with her, and, he had said, she had to stop believing there was.

So maybe, just maybe, inside this suite, alone on what might be the last night of her life, she could reach for a bit of hope.

There was nothing wrong with her, and she didn't know anyone who would want to kill her. No one knew where she was, and no one in this city knew who she was.

She was as safe as she had probably ever been in her entire life.

If something was going to get her, it would have done so already. Or there would be some indication of it.

Maybe her family was just full of it.

Maybe she wasn't going to die after all.

She felt that tiny bit of hope flare. She didn't nurture the flame, though. She set it aside, the way that someone had set hope aside in the mythical Pandora's jar (it was never a box). If Sabrina survived the next 27 hours—and that was a big if—then she would have the freedom—and the free will—to live the life she wanted.

Instead of being afraid of a date far (and then not-so-far) in her future, she would have open sailing. She would live like every other human on the planet (outside of her family).

She would move forward in time, completely oblivious to the fact that she could die at any minute. Or live another sixty-four years, just like her brother. (And see, there she was again—believing the family lore.)

All she had to do was survive the next twenty-seven hours, and everything in her life would change.

Detective Carmen Ramirez hated casino deaths. She had hated guarding the scene when she had been a beat cop, and she hated the deaths even worse now.

The minute she had been assigned a death at the biggest casino complex on The Strip in Las Vegas, she knew she was in for more paperwork than was humanly possible. She would have to go through layers of bureaucracy, and that was just to get inside.

Access would take work, and getting the staff to talk—truly talk—was going to be nearly impossible. Then there was the issue of the press. If the deceased was someone rich or famous, then everything would get even harder. Multiply the problems by a thousand—especially since there would be assistants and agents and some kind of corporation (or corporations) involved.

She scurried down the elevator hallway with the Manager On Duty—a scrawny man with what looked like a permanent frown—as he led her to the marble door that hid the bank of private elevators.

She had been in this part of the hotel more times than she wanted to contemplate. Somehow, she had become Metro's high-end casino detective, the one who knew all the ins and outs handling these unique properties and their problems.

Some of that was because she could handle celebrities and their managers without losing her cool. Some of that was because her closure rate on these kinds of cases was higher than almost all of her colleagues. Some of it was probably personal, as in she had caught some of these cases because she was pretty. She wasn't just making that up, either. Her boss had actually told her that twenty years ago, back when she had been a newly minted detective with absolutely no experience at all.

He believed he needed someone pretty to handle the egos, but she learned it was more than that. Celebrities and their handlers, in particular, seemed to be more comfortable with someone who looked like they had been hired to play a role rather than someone whose life experience was etched all over her face.

That reality could have made her mad. But she had realized long ago that getting angry about things she could not change would hinder her work instead of helping it.

She had enough trouble due to her name and her family's heritage. And the fact that she was shorter than almost everyone else on the force. Being shorter and prettier made a lot of people underestimate her, though, and she often used that to her advantage. That, and she made sure she kept up her fitness training so that if someone tried to mess with her, she could bad-ass them into submission.

The Manager on Duty opened the marble door with a black key card. Rodriguez knew from experience that the key card opened almost everything in this part of the hotel, and was keyed to the MOD. If he lost it or if it was damaged, he had to report it immediately.

Then, he would be suspended without pay for at least 24 hours to ensure no one else accessed off-limits parts of the hotel using his card. If no one did, then he would be reinstated at full salary with a bonus for the time off, as well as an admonition to keep excellent control of his key card at all times.

She had had at least two cases involving key cards at the management level, and she had always been startled at the level of keycard control that the hotel insisted on.

That probably reassured the exceedingly rich clients who booked the part of the hotel she was about to enter, but it certainly seemed complex and baroque to her.

Just like this part of the hotel. Once she and the Manager on Duty went through the marble door, they had a choice of other doors to use. All of them were vaguely color-coded.

The expensive suites—those that cost around three grand a night—had private elevators in a bank through the gray door marked with the room numbers.

That door was to her left, and she had gone through it a number of times.

The villas, which were one gigantic step up from the suites, not only had private elevators, but those elevators were behind private doors, each silver-grayish blue. Those doors were marked with the villa's name. The one she was going to was called The Lucky 77 because it was on the top floor of this wing of the hotel, which was on the seventy-seventh floor.

She refrained from commenting that The Lucky 77 had not been so lucky for the person who had died in the villa. She had also learned that very few people appreciated her propensity for dark humor when she was handling a case. (And some of those people were defense attorneys who said that she did not take her job seriously enough. Of course she took it seriously. She just believed in lightening the load whenever possible.)

Ahead of her was one more door, one she had never accessed. That door was a deep purple that suggested royalty. That door led to the palace level, and that level was gobsmackingly expensive. She knew that some of the most famous celebrities in the world had stayed in those palace rooms, as well as some of the most rich people on Earth.

Those rooms weren't really rooms, but apartments that ran as big as 10,000 square feet, with private pools and entrances and servants at people's beck and call.

She was relieved not to walk through the purple door here.

The villa level, as a different MOD at this property had once told her, was for people who thought themselves rich or who were rich and didn't like throwing away tens of thousands of dollars for an overnight stay.

The palaces were for people who were actually exceedingly rich or people who were exceedingly stupid with what they considered to be a large fortune.

She always remembered what her training officer had told her during her first few days on the job in this city. He had said *You know how to make a small fortune in this town?* And of course, she had shaken her head no. He said with a smile, *You start with a large one.*

She had thought, back then, that he had been cautioning her against gambling, and yes, that was a part of it. But any cop with addictive tendencies was weeded out of Metro long before they headed onto the streets.

But she needed to hear his caution so that she could understand the difference between someone who was so rich that they didn't bother to keep track of ten thousand dollars spent in a single hour and someone who had money (and maybe didn't keep track of it) but couldn't afford to lose ten thousand dollars an hour if they behaved like that over the course of a year.

She wasn't sure she could still spot the difference in those people by sight, but she at least knew that there was quite a range of wealth levels that she would encounter in this city.

She did brace herself, though. The fact that she was

going to a villa and not a palace meant she probably would have fewer hangers-on to deal with, but she might encounter what she privately called one of the asshole wannabes.

Those were the people who earned or inherited more money than she would earn in her entire life and felt that their financial good fortune made them better than she was.

These were her least favorite kinds of people. Even the drug addicts and violent offenders didn't upset her as much as the privileged maybe rich. So, she warned herself as she followed the MOD through one of the private doors to breathe before responding to anyone.

The door led to a small lobby with a handful of chairs pushed against the walls and some tall leafy plants that she couldn't really identify. A side table made of blown glass, with legs that resembled a chubby toddler's, stood between some of the chairs, and a matching vase with lilacs, bright white flowers, and some greenery sat on top.

The lilacs stunk up the entire area and made her nose tickle. She repressed the sneeze as the MOD pressed the elevator button.

She was surprised when the elevator did not open immediately. Then she remembered: there were already a lot of people on scene. She just hoped that the original officers who had caught the call would be savvy enough to lock everything down.

The doors finally opened, and she was able to escape

into a gold and mirrored box that reminded her yet again that no amount of money ensured that designers had good taste.

The doors closed, and she saw herself in the funhouse reflection of their backs. She looked official enough in her blue suit with its matching dress pants, ironed within an inch of their lives. The only thing that screamed police officer (besides the gun she had in a shoulder holster) were the sensible black shoes she wore instead of high heels. Heels would at least have made her reach the MOD's shoulder. Maybe.

He twitched nervously, fingers playing with his key card. He knew he, too, was on the precipice of something that might reflect horribly on his hotel (and him) if he didn't handle the next few hours correctly.

The doors opened into another lobby, which looked like a larger version of the one below. The size meant that the lilacs didn't overpower, but it also meant that two of the officers who had arrived looked smaller than they should have.

It took her a moment to realize that the real reason for that was the mirrored ceiling, with each mirror boxed by gold bars. Gaudy didn't even begin to describe this place.

The officers nodded at her but didn't try to brief her. The officer who had been first on scene had the job of guarding the body to make sure nothing in that room was tampered with.

She had no idea how many officers had responded, but it seemed like there were more than the usual two.

She wended her way through the lobby to the gated entrance. No need for the MOD to use his key card because hotel security stood against the doors, holding them open.

She wondered if that was a good idea. She had a hunch it went against hotel policy.

Another man, dressed in a cheap tuxedo with the hotel's name embroidered along his sleeve, stood near what appeared to be a podium. She had been doing this long enough to realize that it wasn't really a podium, but a butler's table. Still, those things always made her think that the guy in the penguin suit was about to launch into a standup routine in front of a classroom of teenagers.

His gaze met hers; his dark eyes were filled with confusion and disbelief. He had a story to tell. She would get it from him as soon as she could.

She certainly didn't trust one of these officers whom she really didn't know to get a statement correctly.

She passed him and waited at the security gate. It didn't look like a gate. The gate was made of two sliding glass doors with some blue-green etchings on them tinged with gold.

Everything was tinged with gold here. She almost felt like when she left, she would be covered in gold flakes.

The MOD fumbled with his key card, so the butler used

his. She nodded at him, still not saying anything, and stepped into the main entry. It had marble floors flecked with gold leaf and no chairs at all. It was just wide, wasted space, with a few shelves jutting out of the matching gold walls. The shelves were large enough to hold vases, filled with the same arrangement she had seen since she entered the private elevator area.

The smell of lilacs, never one of her favorites, was going to haunt her after this.

The door to the main suite was propped open. A security guard—identifiable by his uniform, his gym muscles, and his look of complete panic—held the door open with his back. He had his arms crossed, and he stared straight ahead, which told her that the crime scene—wherever it was—was not something he really wanted to look at.

She slipped past him. The main room (she had no idea what to call it) was sunken, so she had to take two steps down to reach any furniture. Just past the white and gold sofas and easy chairs, the white and gold rug, and the end tables that had the same blown-glass baby-legs design as the one in the private lobby, were a circular bar made of some kind of gold something or other, with matching gold chairs, and more liquor than she had seen on display at her favorite neighborhood place.

Despite what she had seen from the security guard, there was no one in this big room at all. Not one of her officers either, which annoyed her. Someone should have been out here, keeping an eye on this room.

She probably didn't have enough staff, which annoyed her even more.

She walked across the room, careful not to step on the rug. Instead, she walked along the second step down which went all the way to another set of open glass doors. From those, she could just see the private pool. There were white and gold chairs near it, but before she got to it, she would have to walk through the dining area, which had a white table that seated eight, with white chairs all around it.

She didn't see blood.

She didn't see any evidence of a crime at all.

Someone should have briefed her. Someone should have been out here taking her in and letting her know what was going on.

She was about to pick up her radio when she heard voices ahead of her. She walked toward them through the glass doors. The doors, even partially open, blocked sound, which surprised her.

As she passed them, the voices got louder.

"...call a lawyer," a woman said.

"That's your prerogative, Miss."

Rodriguez recognized the flat tone of a police officer, although she didn't recognize the man's voice at all.

"I called *you!*" The woman's voice was thick with tears.

"Yes, you did, Miss," the officer said.

"I don't think you can legally hold me here," she said.

It sounded like everything was about to escalate, so

Rodriguez stopped looking closely at the scene and stepped deeper into the next room.

It wasn't a formal living room, which was what she sort of expected. It was more like a family room as reimagined by someone with too much gold leaf. There was a large fireplace against the wall that looked like a real fireplace. The fireplace frame was shiny gold, as was the tile floor in front of the fireplace, and the fireplace tools, some of which had spilled onto that floor.

The spilled tools were the first mess she had seen since she arrived.

The voices had stopped. She expected that their owners were watching her. So, she took her time turning toward them.

A large screen TV covered one wall. In front of the other wall stood a woman wearing a flowing overlayer made of multicolored gauze. It almost looked like she was wearing layered scarves over some blue tights.

But those weren't really tights. They were more of a dancer's leotard because they went all the way up to her neck. Sleeves ran down her arms. Her fingers were covered in rings, some of which were tarnished.

She wore ballet flats that were worn along the edges.

She didn't belong in this room.

Next to her stood one of the officers, a beat cop Rodriguez recognized from other investigations she had done on the Strip. He was pushing sixty, but was trim as a person could be because he insisted on walking the length of the Strip at least once every day he was on duty.

He was competent, thoughtful, and smart.

"Officer Weaver," she said, not quite letting the pleasure she felt at his presence in her voice.

"Detective Rodriguez," he said, deliberately not introducing the gauzy woman next to him.

"What are we looking at here?" Rodriguez said. "I was sent before anyone could brief me."

"My partner will show you," Weaver said. It was all telegraphs and signals. *My partner will show you* meant that he didn't want to leave the gauze-woman's side for some reason.

The partner peered out of an adjoining room. He was young, with bright red hair that wanted to curl despite his short haircut. Rodriguez didn't recognize him. Weaver was probably training people again.

"Detective," the young officer said. His porcelain skin looked even paler than usual.

Rodriguez shot the gauze-woman another glance. The woman wouldn't meet her eyes. She was looking down at her hands, which were folded in front of her.

Then Rodriguez walked past the gauze-woman and Weaver toward the partner.

She smelled it before she got there, the heavy scent of blood. There was a tinge of vomit too, but it seemed to come from a room that she was passing without even realizing it—a gigantic bathroom suite, which was divided into sections. She could only see a large tub, with unlit candles along its side, and a bird's eye view of Las Vegas.

The vomit smell must have been very strong in the toilet area, which she couldn't see. No one had flushed, so someone was afraid of contaminating a crime scene.

Past that door was the source of the blood smell.

The white-and-gold rug underneath an overlarge bed was covered in blood spatter, as was the gold tile floor that led into the bathroom. The chairs along the far wall—a wall with the same view of the city as the bathroom—looked untouched.

For a moment, Rodriguez didn't see the body at all, and then she noticed the feet pointing downward on the floor beside the bed. Those feet were bare, as were the legs they were attached to.

They were also large and bony. They were pale, and not covered in blood. The calves weren't either nor were the back of the knees.

She couldn't see beyond that.

But she could tell that there were no bloody footprints leading away from the body or leading toward it, in case whoever it was that had died had walked through some blood on the way to collapse.

The partner was standing just behind the door, cataloguing spatter. The gold leaf wall near him was covered with it.

A fireplace poker had been tossed perpendicular to the

wall. Both parts of the poker—the curled sharp point and the pointed edge above it—were black with blood.

"I'm Detective Rodriguez," she said without stepping closer to the partner.

"I figured," the partner said. "Weaver asked for you specifically."

That made sense, actually, considering how many times they had worked together. But it also meant that Weaver thought this murder was going to be a tricky one.

It might not be a tricky one to solve, but it would be a tricky one to prosecute.

"I'm Shaun Michaels, but everyone calls me Red."

For obvious reasons, clearly.

"All right, Red," Rodriguez said. "Walk me through this."

"If only I could," Red said. "I've been instructed not to move until the ME gets here. "

She almost smiled. Weaver was a good cop. She could hear him giving that instruction.

"From where you are, then," she said.

"Okay." Red cleared his throat. "You'll have to be careful where you walk."

She loved those first instructions. They usually were the ones that the person speaking had violated.

"The blood spatter disappears on that tile." Red pointed to a heel print near the door. "Unfortunately, that one is mine."

And maybe the smell of vomit? She wanted to ask but didn't. Because Red's face was beginning to match his name. Clearly he was being trained and this was probably his very first bloody murder scene.

"Um," he said, clearing his throat. Yep, the vomit was his. "There's a lot on the walls here. Weaver thinks that's where the guy got hit first."

"Okay, no opinions right now," Rodriguez said. "Just tell me what you know."

"There's a lot of spatter, and the fireplace poker is covered in blood. There's a smear near it, which tells me that it was tossed over there." His flush got darker. "Sorry, detective. No opinions. It's just that I've had some time to think this over."

"I appreciate that, officer," she said. "It's okay to point out things. Even okay to tell me how you think they're connected, but don't tell me how you think this crime was committed."

"Yes, ma'am." He nodded, as if he was used to being reprimanded. "Anyway, the lady out there—." He waved his hand toward the gauze-woman. "She said the body was in here. Those were her words, ma'am."

Rodriguez wasn't sure how she had gone from "detective" to "ma'am," but she would take it. As far as she was concerned, that was a step up in respect.

"So I came in first…" Which was probably where he made his mistake. "…and blundered toward that side of the bed…" Yep. That confirmed her assumption.

It also added another: he was a good kid, but he was very green.

"…and then I saw him. He doesn't have much of a head, ma'am." Red urped, the way people did when they were about to puke. But he managed to hold it down.

Rodriguez waited for Red to get control of his voice again.

"And, um, he's naked, ma'am. His clothes aren't anywhere to be seen."

Fascinating on both details.

When she realized that Red wasn't going to say anything more, she asked, "Anything else?"

"No, ma'am. Officer Weaver stopped me before I got too deep into the crime scene, ma'am."

This time, Rodriguez was unable to prevent a smile. Of course, Weaver prevented Red from doing anything else. The kid might have contaminated the crime scene already.

She was going to have to be careful, too. The fact that there was spatter everywhere meant she was going to have to tread lightly.

"Any ETA on the coroner's office?" she asked Red.

He shrugged. "I've been in here and haven't heard any chatter. But we've been here for more than forty minutes now. You'd think they would have gotten to the scene quicker."

She didn't join in the criticism. Simply traversing the length of this gigantic hotel complex took a while. Ambulances had to park in a special area, and unless the deceased was in a public location, the EMTs had to use the service elevators.

It was the same for police in uniform and the coroner's office. There was no need for patrons of this place, where they were supposed to be having fun, to see the ugly downside of life.

She reached into her pocket and removed a pair of booties. She put one over her practical shoes, then set her foot down, and slid the other bootie over her other shoe. She still wasn't going to traipse into the main part of the crime scene, but at least if she picked up any trace, she would be able to give it to the crime scene analysts.

Rodriguez eased her way around Red, careful to stay off the tile, and peered around the bed.

The scene became clearer from this angle. The victim, an adult male, was sprawled on his stomach, hands beside his head—or what remained of his head—palms down, as if he had tried to catch himself when he fell.

Red wasn't exactly right in his description. The head wasn't missing, but it no longer looked like a head. The back was incredibly flat and sprawled, with brain matter and blackish residue that was probably coagulating blood.

More spatter ran along the side of the bed and upwards toward the nightstand. And there were, for lack of a better term, skitter marks that led to the fireplace poker.

Whoever had used it—and she would be surprised if it wasn't the actual weapon—had tossed it away, and it had slid across the tile floor to its final position.

What surprised her was that the blood looked like it

was congealing, even in the big pool where the body rested. The skitter marks were more black than red.

The profound odor of blood in the room was actually a sign that the smell had been there for a while. Although that surprised her too—not that the body had been here for awhile, but that the smell lingered.

Someone had shut off the HVAC system, at least in this room. It was a bit stuffy, and that was unusual in any modern indoor space in Las Vegas. Opening windows in the desert was a bad idea—every place would get filled with sand. So, the air got filtered through some truly impressive HVAC systems.

She didn't know how the air filtration worked in this part of the hotel. She suspected the system was isolated to each villa so that if a neighbor were using their fireplace or vaping, the smell wouldn't cross into someone else's personal space.

More things to find out. Right now, she was not taking notes. She wouldn't start doing that for a while, because she wanted the crime scene analysts to make their judgments without prejudice, just like she would do.

She eased her way back to the door. Red was still cataloguing and probably had a bit more knowledge about the scene, but she didn't want to talk with him.

She needed to talk to Weaver.

She came out of the door. Weaver was still standing next to the gauze-woman, who was hunched over, face in her hands.

"I need to talk to you," Rodriguez said. "Can anyone else…?"

She waved a hand at the gauze-woman, since she didn't want to mention the woman at all.

"Yeah." He used his radio and asked another officer to come into the room. That officer came from a different part of the villa, closer to the pool, part of the large space that Rodriguez had not yet visited.

She walked to the bar, trusting Weaver to follow. From this spot, she could see a few other officers near the pool and one in what looked like a butler's kitchen, all of them photographing and cataloguing while they waited for the crime scene analysts.

"Who is the woman?" Rodriguez asked as soon as Weaver reached her side.

"She's the only name on the room. Sabrina Greenwald. Booked the villa a month ago. Says no one came here with her, and no one knew she was here."

Rodriguez nodded. "What else did you get from her?"

"Not much," he said. "She's the one that called it in, but she didn't want anyone in the room until police arrived. She said that she 'thought' he was dead."

"If she had doubt, then she's the only one," Rodriguez said.

Weaver's mouth was in a thin line. He glanced at the gauze-woman, whom Rodriguez had better start thinking of as Greenwald, and then back at Rodriguez.

"You're going to have some difficulty with this one," he said, his voice low. "She doesn't fit here."

That was obvious just from the way she dressed. The leotard she was wearing underneath the gauzy stuff looked thin in some places. Her shoes weren't expensive, and her hair was in desperate need of a cut.

Rodriguez had seen celebrities and wealthier clients who dressed like that, but the shoes were usually a give-away, no matter what someone's mental state or desire to hide.

Gauze-woman...um, Greenwald...wore shoes that should have been thrown out a long time ago.

"She give you any indication why she's here?" Rodriguez asked.

"No," Weaver said, but he looked a bit uncertain. "She did say that she expected to die today."

"So, she defended herself against this man?" Rodriguez asked.

"That's where it gets hazy, and honestly, when questioning people gets hazy, I think it's better if the detective on the case does it."

That was one of the things she loved about working with Weaver. He knew how to hold onto boundaries.

"Thank you," Rodriguez said.

Weaver nodded. "You need to know that she's really skittish. She backed away from me when I came over to interview her. Then, when she decided that I was trustworthy, she wouldn't let me out of her sight."

He glanced over at her, and Rodriguez did the same. The gauze-woman was watching them through parted fingers.

She did look skittish. But skittishness was a normal response to an assault.

Although something felt wrong here.

"What else can you tell me?" Rodriguez asked.

"A couple things," Weaver said. "The timeline looks off."

She had noticed that too, but she wanted him to tell it. "Meaning?"

"She called 911 less than an hour ago. He's been dead a lot longer than that. That's obvious from the blood pool."

And the spatter and the stains and the smell. But Rodriguez didn't say any of those things.

"Yeah," she said.

"The butler outside is supposed to be at his desk at all times, unless the client wants him to attend to something."

Rodriguez knew that. She had worked up here before. But she didn't mind the refresher.

"This client wanted him to leave the desk and not return, but he can't do that. Hotel regulations."

"He told you that?" Rodriguez asked.

"No." Weaver was barely speaking above a whisper. "He told one of my guys. Then he said that he had no idea that there was a man in this villa, let alone someone she would have gotten naked with."

"We're assuming she wanted to get naked with the dead man?" Rodriguez asked. She kept a sideways gaze on the gauze-woman. She didn't seem like someone who would show up for a tryst, but she might have.

That would explain the shoes. If the dead guy was the one who actually paid for the room, but put it under her name, then her obvious lack of high-end funds made sense.

"Right now, we're not assuming much. But our butler assumed it, and he thought he would have known."

"Was there any time he was away from his desk, maybe on an errand for her?" Rodriguez asked.

"He's allowed a ten-minute break every hour to attend to personal things, like getting a snack, using the bathroom. During that break, another butler is supposed to replace him. He said that about three hours ago, he had a personal bathroom emergency and had to leave before his replacement showed up, but he timed it, and the desk was only unmanned for maybe two or three minutes."

Two or three minutes was long enough for someone to sneak into the room or sneak out of the room.

"We're going to need the security video from that private entry," she said. "And the elevator, and the private lobby."

"Already ordered it," Weaver said. "I sent two officers to the security room to make sure nothing was deleted or destroyed."

This often happened when the accused or the deceased was someone famous. Las Vegas Metro had many, many, many systems in place to prevent just such an occurrence.

"Great, thank you." She actually expected no less from

Weaver, but she had to check. "What else turned up in your sweep of the villa?"

He was prepared to answer that too. "We didn't find anyone else here. The second bedroom doesn't even look like it was used. No clothes in the closet, nothing."

"I sense a 'but,'" she said.

He gave her a small knowing smile. "Yeah," he said. "The clothes in the main bedroom are all hers. However, there's a pile of clothes and some men's shoes on the bathroom floor, near the shower."

Probably not too far from where Red lost the entire contents of his stomach.

"You're assuming those clothes belong to the victim," she said.

"Yep, but that's for the analysts to decide." Weaver nodded toward the woman. "What do you want to do there?"

"Do you have any female officers?" Rodriguez asked. It was protocol to have a second officer present for a preliminary interview, and since there was possibly a sexual component to this murder, it would be best to have two women talking to the suspect.

It was interesting to her that she had gone from thinking of the gauze woman as a person to a suspect. Rodriguez didn't have any evidence yet, just a lot of circumstantial events.

"I have a female officer. I'll send her over." Weaver's

frown eased a bit. "She's been doing this job a long time. She was on scene with that horrific stabbing in 2022."

Some random crazy lost what was left of his mind that summer and ran down the Strip, stabbing anyone who got in his way. Two people died and six more were seriously injured.

The beat officers on the scene stopped him quickly and prevented more injuries, but it was a horrific attack, one that made whatever happened here look like child's play.

"That sounds good," Rodriguez said. "And, someone needs to stick with the butler. Let's get the hotel security off the door and place them down in the elevator lobby. The Manager on Duty doesn't need to be here either." She hadn't seen any other employees. "Unless that security officer came up here first...?"

"No," Weaver said. "Our officers were first on scene."

"All right, then," Rodriguez said. "Let's get this scene locked down."

He nodded and left her.

She squared her shoulders. She would wait until the female officer arrived. In the meantime, Rodriguez kept an eye on the gauze-woman. She remained hunched, hands over her face. She wasn't quite rocking back and forth, but she wasn't far away from doing so either.

She didn't look entirely sane. But then, no one would if they had just killed a man.

Or if they had been attacked.

She shook the assumptions out of her head. For all she

knew, this Greenwald woman returned from lunch or a shopping trip, came up to the villa to find the man dead in the bedroom.

The female officer reached her side. The officer was tall and lanky, with a deep tan and sun lines all over her face. Her eyes were dark and serious.

Rodriguez recognized her, but for the life of her, couldn't remember the woman's first name. The brass-colored name tag that was part of her uniform helpfully identified her as L. Piña.

"Officer Piña, I'll need you to take notes," Rodriguez said. "I'd like you to record the interview as well."

Piña reached into her jacket pocket and pulled out a small notepad. She also grabbed her phone.

Rodriguez grabbed hers as well. There would be two recordings of this conversation because she had learned the hard way that trusting someone else wasn't always the best idea.

"We're going to approach carefully," she said softly. "I'm not sure what we're dealing with here."

"Yes, ma'am," Piña said.

Rodriguez walked slowly across the expanse of the den, or whatever this room was called, until she reached Greenwald's side. The woman smelled strongly of flop sweat. She was leaning on a bolster pillow that someone had placed on the floor, and she was sitting cross-legged, which Rodriguez hadn't expected.

She had thought all this time that Greenwald was crouching.

Greenwald moved her hands and looked up at Rodriguez. Right now, Rodriguez was towering over her, which was a strange position for Rodriguez, of all people, to be in.

"Ms. Greenwald," Rodriguez said as gently as she could. "I'm Detective Carmen Rodriguez. I'd like to talk with you, but I don't want to do it like this. Can we move to some chairs?"

"I'm fine here," Greenwald said. She grabbed the bolster with both hands, as if holding it in place.

"Yes, but I'm looming right now," Rodriguez said, "and that's not going to be comfortable for either of us."

Greenwald shook her head. "There's too many people here. I can't...I can't..." Her voice trailed off.

"You can't what?" Rodriguez asked.

"I can't sit anywhere. I need to be able to see what they're doing."

The level of fear rising from that woman made her voice shake. Rodriguez had dealt with this before.

"If we move chairs against one of the walls behind you, will that work?"

Greenwald swallowed. "I don't know," she said.

"We'll have to work behind you to do it, unless you want to help...?" Rodriguez kept her voice soft so that she wouldn't give any orders. Not yet anyway.

Greenwald sighed. Then she stood up, clutching the bolster in front of herself as if it was a shield.

She turned slightly sideways so that her back was to one of the corners, where no one was. She could see most of the room from that position.

"Go ahead," she said as if she was the one in charge. Only her voice was too wispy to be in charge. "I'll sit against that wall."

She pointed to the one directly behind her. It was the only one with a view of all the doors and open spaces.

"Officer Piña, if you don't mind," Rodriguez said. "I'll stay here with Ms. Greenwald."

"Sabrina," Greenwald said. "Please. Sabrina. Ms. Green-wald is my mother."

Rodriguez understood that complaint. She'd heard it often enough in her own head. It was one of the stranger parts of growing older that other people saw you so very differently from the way you saw yourself.

"Sabrina, then," Rodriguez said.

Piña was moving some heavy wooden chairs to the wall. They had been around the dining room table. They had thick padding on both the seats and the backs, and they were so pristine white that Rodriguez almost objected.

And then she changed her mind. It was good that they were white. If there was trace on Greenwald's clothing, it would show up on the chair immediately.

She finally finished setting up. Rodriguez thanked her

and then led Greenwald to the chairs. Rodriguez did not touch Greenwald in any way and kept a rather large personal distance between them.

Greenwald picked a chair as close to the corner as she could get. That way, two walls protected her, although if she was truly afraid someone would come for her, the two walls and the chair on the other side made it almost impossible for her to flee. She would be trapped there.

She clearly wasn't a strategic thinker.

But Rodriguez wasn't going to box Greenwald in. Rodriguez picked the chair next to her but moved it away from Greenwald slightly and turned it toward her so that Rodriguez could face her rather than sit beside her.

Piña took the farthest chair from Greenwald and sat in it sideways so that she could see both Rodriguez and Greenwald at the same time. Piña had a notebook on her lap and a pen in her hand.

Greenwald flitted her eyes at Piña, clearly noting what Piña was doing. Then Greenwald bowed her head again and looked at her hands.

Her posture gave Rodriguez a chance to look her over. If her clothing had been stained with a lot of blood, it would have been easy to see. But Rodriguez hadn't seen a major blood stain at all, but that didn't mean there wasn't spatter.

However, the flowing colors on gauzy scarf-like things that Greenwald wore over the leotard made it almost impossible to see anything small or smeared.

"Can I get you anything?" Rodriguez asked. "Something to drink, maybe?"

Greenwald shook her head, but she didn't raise it. She kept her hands tightly clasped together. She had shoved them between her knees, so Rodriguez couldn't really get a good look at them.

"All right, then," Rodriguez said. "Please let me know if you need anything at all. Food, water, a bathroom, maybe."

She waited so that the offer sounded sincere. It was sincere. She didn't mind tending to this woman in the short term, if it got answers out of her.

Rodriguez let the silence hang for a moment, conscious that if she let it hang too long, she would seem manipulative.

"All right," Rodriguez said gently. "I'm here to find out what happened today."

Greenwald nodded, but still didn't lift her head. She hunched even more than she had a moment ago.

Rodriguez was about to try a different tactic when Greenwald bowed her head deeper.

"I...can't stay here..." she said so softly that it was almost inaudible.

Rodriguez had to lean in. She deliberately clasped her hands together, mirroring Greenwald's posture just a little, and hoped it was enough to seem sympathetic.

"Where would you like us to take you?" Rodriguez asked gently.

Greenwald shook her head and collapsed even more. "I

don't know," she said, her voice thick with tears. "I don't know. Somewhere without people."

She had come to the wrong city for that. In fact, she was in the wrong place in the wrong city. More than 100,000 people visited the Strip every day, and even more were scattered throughout all the businesses, hoping to serve those people.

Each hotel was a small city, and Greenwald had chosen one of the larger hotels. There was no telling how many people she would see just trying to leave the building.

"Is that why you booked this villa?" Rodriguez asked. "To avoid people?"

It was large. Greenwald would have had about three thousand square feet of privacy here, if she wanted it.

"Yeah," Greenwald said ever so quietly. "Yeah, but then..."

And she stopped. She was skittish and in tears, but she seemed to be in control of her faculties. She hadn't reached that stage yet where her emotions had overtaken her reason.

"Then...?" Rodriguez asked.

Greenwald lifted her head. Her face was tear-streaked, but she wasn't wearing makeup. And, it appeared, there was a smudge of blood along her chin, and some droplets on her neck.

"I'm supposed to die today," she said.

Rodriguez hadn't expected the *supposed to* and the present tense. She had thought, when Weaver said something about this, that Greenwald had been afraid she was going to die, which would have suggested, somehow, that the attack on the naked man was self-defense.

"Supposed to?" Rodriguez repeated.

Greenwald nodded. "I have to get through the day. We can talk if I get through the day."

Rodriguez sat up. "So, someone is trying to kill you?"

"I don't know," Greenwald said. "Maybe. But maybe…"

She stopped again. It was almost as if she had some kind of cutoff in her head, something that made her suspect she was saying too much.

"If someone is trying to kill you," Rodriguez said, "then we need to get you somewhere safe. We can protect you."

Greenwald was shaking her head. "If I go somewhere with people, there's a chance that something can go wrong. I might die."

The comment felt off. Someone who knew they had been targeted usually wanted to go to a safe place.

"Going to the station would be safe," Rodriguez said.

Greenwald was still shaking her head. "It's not safe. Nowhere is safe. I just have to get through the day."

"What's so special about the day?" Rodriguez asked.

Greenwald stopped shaking her head. She faced Rodriguez for the first time. Greenwald's blue eyes were almost clear. They were rimmed by very dark and long black lashes, making her eyes seem almost colorless.

That gave her a slightly eerie look, deeply unsettling.

Greenwald let out a small laugh. Her black eyebrows

went downward in a frown at the same time, and she started shaking her head again.

"It's impossible," she said, and this time her voice had more force. "It's…if I talk to you, you'll think I'm crazy. If I don't and hire a lawyer, then I'm planning for the future, a future I probably won't have. If I don't say anything, no one will know what happened, but I'm not sure it matters exactly what happened. I think we just need to get through the day, and I'll talk to you tomorrow."

Greenwald was right. The more she talked, the more Rodriguez thought she was crazy.

"So…" Rodriguez said slowly, thinking this through. Her training told her to let the subject decide what to discuss. "If we don't talk today, what do you plan to do now?"

She heard a faint shuffling behind her. That had to be Piña who probably hadn't expected this line of questioning.

Greenwald's expression changed ever so slightly. Her panic seemed to ease just a little bit.

"I need to get another room, maybe here in the hotel. Since I paid so much, do you think they'll move me?" She sounded both clueless and hopeful at the same time.

And she answered one of Rodriguez's main questions: whether or not Greenwald had paid for the room. She had. As upset as she was, she would have said something else if the dead guy had paid—anything from "given how much he paid" to "how much *we* paid."

"I don't know," Rodriguez said. She didn't add that the

police would need her in the short term, and the hotel would want to know what happened here before they moved anyone.

"Maybe the butler knows. God, I'm usually not like this. I learn people's names, like, the first thing. I listen to them, I figure them out. And he—well, I remember his death day. It's in January forty-five years from now, but can I remember his name? No, of course not."

She was chattering as if some kind of dam had broken. She started to stand.

"Let's go ask him. He said he can do whatever I need. And I haven't needed anything until now."

She looked almost hopeful, as if this was the answer to all of her problems.

Rodriguez held up a hand, not in a flat-out palm position as in *stop*, but more like she was halfway between physically stopping Greenwald and asking her to stop herself.

"Not yet," Rodriguez said. "The other officers are talking with him. Please sit with me a moment longer."

All the hope drained from Greenwald's face. She sank back into the chair and hunched again, not as far forward as she had earlier, but quite a bit, almost like she was protecting her torso.

"You asked what I want to do," Greenwald said, almost sounding like a petulant child. "I would like to move rooms."

"I understand," Rodriguez said. "And we will see how

we can accommodate that, but while we're waiting for him to finish with the other officers, let's finish our discussion."

Greenwald's mouth thinned. "I—there's nothing to say until I get safe."

Rodriguez could approach the conversation in two different ways. She could grab one of the nuggets Greenwald tossed at her during the mention of the butler, or she could focus on the other important aspect of what Greenwald was saying.

"May I ask," Rodriguez said, remembering to be as gentle as she could, "what makes you feel unsafe in this villa?"

Most people would snap, *You mean besides the dead guy in the bedroom?* But Greenwald lifted her chin and sat up just a little.

"I'm not safe anywhere today," she said. "I'm supposed to die today."

And that was when both lines of questioning combined.

"You mentioned the butler's name, but you knew his death day," Rodriguez said. "What do you mean by that?"

Greenwald's face suffused with color and she closed her eyes tightly, the way that people did when they knew they had made some kind of mistake.

"I didn't mean anything," she said as she opened her eyes. "I didn't."

"Is this your death day?" Rodriguez asked.

Greenwald looked completely panicked now. "I'm supposed to die today," she said again.

"Says who?" Rodriguez asked, and this time she refrained from adding, *we can protect you.*

"All the portents," Greenwald said. "Everything from my birth forward said I was going to die today."

The pieces started falling into place. Rodriguez had to tread very carefully on this one. "And the butler will die in January, forty-five years from now."

Greenwald nodded.

"You ran his...portents?" It was hard to choose the right word. She was worried about losing the thread of this conversation.

"No," Greenwald said. "That's not how it works."

"How does it work?" Rodriguez was having a very difficult time controlling her tone. She wanted to sound empathetic. She wanted Greenwald to believe that Rodriguez was on her side. But getting into this make-believe magic crap reminded Rodriguez of her college roommate who was always asking the tarot cards about each and every decision or her grandmother who lived her life according to every superstition known to man.

Greenwald opened her mouth and then closed it. Her expression changed again. It went from needy to knowing.

"I won't be able to convince you," she said.

"You're not supposed to convince me," Rodriguez said. "I'm here to learn the facts. This is a fact."

For you, she barely kept herself from adding. *This is a fact for you.*

"I shook his hand," Greenwald said. "I didn't want to. It

just happened. You know how people introduce themselves and offer a hand for you to grab? He did that, and I was distracted by this place. It's so gaudy. I hadn't expected it to be so gaudy, and then he said he was the butler and he would be at my beck and call, which was exactly what I didn't want, and then he extended his hand while I was thinking about how to get rid of him, and said his name and as he did, I knew: He was going to die in forty-five years. In January. The twelfth. But I didn't tell him. Most people don't want to know, and I really, really, really understand why."

"If I give you my hand, you can tell me when I will die?" Rodriguez said.

"I won't do it," Greenwald said. "It's a terrible thing to live with."

"That's what you're living with now," Rodriguez said. They were speaking softly. Piña had actually moved closer.

Rodriguez wanted to signal her to stay back. She didn't want anyone volunteering for this kind of weirdness.

"Yes," Greenwald said cautiously. "Today is my death day."

The words hung between them. Rodriguez was beginning to get a sense of what was happening here, but she didn't want to make assumptions.

"You have always known the date, but not the time of day?" Rodriguez asked.

"That's right," Greenwald said.

"And I assume you know the location," Rodriguez said.

"No," Greenwald said, "and that's part of the problem. If you think about it, the more information you have, the easier it would be to avoid. But I guess we're not supposed to avoid it. I mean, I've lived my entire life worrying about this day, and now it's here."

Rodriguez wanted to judge the level of crazy before she went too deep into the rest of this.

And, she silently reprimanded herself, she had to make herself stop thinking about any of this as crazy. Because she wouldn't be empathize if she was being too obviously judgmental.

"Okay," Rodriguez said. "One thing I need to clarify. You were born with this ability, right?"

"Every woman in my family has it," Greenwald said.

And if every woman told someone it was their death day, did they facilitate that death with the knowledge, forcing that person into risky behavior or did they keep it to themselves?

Rodriguez was a bit surprised at those kinds of questions floating through her head. She was fascinated by this, and she didn't want to be.

"So, you knew, when you were born, what day you were going to die on?" Rodriguez asked.

"I can't remember a time when I didn't know," Greenwald said.

"Was your ability that told you this?" Rodriguez asked. "Or did someone in your family tell?"

"I don't know," Greenwald said.

"But you do know the death dates of others," Rodriguez asked.

"I don't want to, but it's true, yes." Greenwald raised her chin. She was actually a bit defiant, which made sense. If she had been telling people she could do this for her entire life, and they pushed back, she would be defensive from the get-go.

"And have some of those death days come about already?" Rodriguez asked.

"Yeah." Greenwald breathed the word. There was pain in it.

"Were you surprised by any of those deaths?"

Her eyes filled with tears. "Everyone in my best friend's family. Everyone. Car accident twenty years ago. April 14. They were goofing around and no one wore seatbelts and who the hell believes a ten-year-old when she realizes that everyone is going to die? My grandmother told them first, and they refused to let us in their house ever again. But Angie, my friend, she and I still saw each other, just not at home, and then, she just—they just—it was awful."

Rodriguez nodded. "It sounds awful."

She wanted to add *Was that the only one?* But she didn't. She didn't have the time to do a full-ranging interview. The scene was already changing around them.

The crime scene analysts had arrived with their big boxes of gear. They were wearing their white Tyvek suits that made little whispering sounds as they walked. They tried to be silent, but they weren't.

If the evidence took them out here, then Rodriguez would have to move this interview, and that was the last thing she wanted to do. It was working right now, and she wanted to keep it going.

"How do people respond when they learn about their death day?" Rodriguez asked.

Greenwald's mouth thinned. She glanced at the parade of crime scene analysts, then looked back at Rodriguez, almost as if she felt the ticking clock too.

"Sometimes they laugh. Sometimes they make fun of me. Sometimes they try to avoid it. Sometimes they want to find out about all of their friends—and of course, I don't tell them that." As if she had standards, and she probably did.

"How has your family responded to yours?" Rodriguez asked.

"They wanted me to stay home." The tears were back in Greenwald's eyes. She wiped at them angrily. "They wanted me to spend the last days with them."

"But you didn't," Rodriguez said.

"I didn't want them to die, too." Greenwald waved her hand. "Like that poor man."

And then she caught herself and gasped.

"He was collateral damage?" Rodriguez asked.

"I shouldn't say anymore," Greenwald said.

And here was the tightrope. Every interview had one, and it was always a surprise. If the interviewer didn't handle it well, then the moment would be lost forever. Or it would taint a legal case. Or it might let a murderer go free.

Rodriguez knew all of that, and she knew she had to set it aside. But she had to be aware that the tightrope existed.

"If indeed this is your actual death day," Rodriguez said, "then you could die at any moment."

"Yes." Greenwald sounded sullen.

"You're not sick, right?" Rodriguez asked. "No long-term diseases?"

"Yeah, no, none. I'm healthy," Greenwald said.

"So the death, if you hadn't known about the day, it would have been unexpected. To you and your family. Like that awful car accident." Rodriguez was keeping her tone measured. It took a lot of work to do so.

"Yeah." Greenwald frowned.

Rodriguez could almost hear the *so?* tacked onto the defensive *yeah*.

"Well," Rodriguez said, "if I take you at your word—and I am—then you won't be here tomorrow."

Most people would be slightly taken aback by that statement, especially if what Greenwald was doing was fabricating a hell of a lie.

But Greenwald continued to frown and give Rodriguez a slightly suspicious side-eye.

"And if you're not planning to be here, then you have some vital information about what happened in this room, information we're not going to be able to get from anyone else."

That was the test. Did this woman actually believe she was going to die? Or was she a con artist with a great story? Or was she just plain old nuts?

"I don't need to help you do your job," Greenwald said.

Strike one on the true believer theory. If Greenwald actually believed she was going to die, what did it matter if she helped Rodriguez do the job or not?

But Rodriguez couldn't get defensive. Part of her—a rather large part of her, truth be told—thought that Greenwald believed her wild story.

It explained the expensive hotel suite, for one, especially since she couldn't afford it. Or it was a push for her.

Of course, there were other things that would explain the room, but Rodriguez was going to set them aside for the moment.

"I'm more concerned with that man's family," Rodriguez said. "If you die today, they'll never understand what happened to him."

"I don't need to care about him," Greenwald said, but her voice shook.

"I'm not asking you to care about him," Rodriguez said. "I'm asking you to think of his family."

"The people who created that monster," Greenwald said.

Rodriguez waited, biting back half a dozen responses that she would use in a traditional interview. *How did you know he's a monster? What happened between the two of you? Did you know him before?*

Silence, though. Sometimes that was the interviewer's best tool. And despite the constant movement of the crime scene analysts and the faint sound of their discussions from the bedroom, Rodriguez held Greenwald's gaze.

"I don't know them," Greenwald said. "I have no obligation to anyone."

Except the family you left behind, who either believe that you're crazy and think that you need supervision, or who are very worried about you since they think you're going to die.

(Or, a tiny voice in Rodriguez's head added, you have no family, no one cares about you, and you accidentally killed someone in the middle of a larger scam.)

"He was naked, for godssake!" Greenwald said. "He came into my place and he disrobed and he went to my bedroom and he was going to hurt me. He was going to attack me and have his way with me—"

That was an old-fashioned way of putting it. Rodriguez forced herself to focus, though.

"—and then he was going to kill me. So I had no choice." Greenwald's voice lowered. "I had no choice."

"Who was he?" Rodriguez asked.

"I don't know!" Greenwald's voice went up. "They said it was safe up here, and then that strange butler let him in. Or someone did. Because he just strode in here like he owned the place and went into the bathroom."

"Then what?" Rodriguez asked, concentrating hard. The other questions, like *Why didn't you leave? Why didn't you call hotel security?* could wait for a different interview.

"I grabbed the poker to defend myself. I needed him out of here. I was going to tell him that, and then..." She stopped and closed her eyes.

Rodriguez kept waiting. Waiting was working so far, so she didn't want to mess with that.

"And then...I don't know. I was just so scared."

She opened her eyes. As ridiculous as this sounded, Rodriguez was beginning to believe her.

But Greenwald didn't say anything else. She kept her lips pressed together.

Rodriguez couldn't suggest the next part. She didn't dare. Because *she* didn't believe that Greenwald was going to die today, and that meant Rodriguez had to do all of this with an eye to the case ahead.

"I bet you were," Rodriguez said with as much compassion as she could muster. "You finally had your answer as to what was going to happen today."

"Yeah." That single word was breathy again. Greenwald bit her lower lip. "Yeah, I thought I had the answer."

"But that wasn't the answer, was it?" Rodriguez said. "Unless it was, and you changed your destiny...?"

Greenwald let out a small sigh. "I thought—I've always thought—I would just let it happen, you know. But I realized I didn't want to go out badly. I just wanted it to be over, you know? To end, if it was going to end."

Rodriguez nodded.

"But he was naked and I knew—I knew—my last

53

memories were going to be something awful, and I just had to—I mean, maybe it'll reset, you know?"

"Maybe what will reset?" Rodriguez asked.

"I mean, maybe the death's not fixed," Greenwald said, "but maybe the death date *is*, does that make sense?"

Or maybe we just don't know our death date, and this is all a bunch of crap, Rodriguez thought. It was getting harder and harder to have any empathy for this woman.

But she said, "Let me see if I understand this. You think the method of death might change depending on where the person is, but that they might die on that day no matter what?"

Greenwald bit her lower lip as she nodded.

"That's what I'm afraid of," she said softly.

Rodriguez had no idea how to respond to that. She reached for her training: When interviewing a crazy person, you had to step briefly into their worldview, but you couldn't live there.

Greenwald was looking at her hands again. Rodriguez gave them a good look as well, and noted that the nails were cut short. There was no blood underneath them.

In fact, there was no blood at all on Greenwald's hands, and there would have been if she had used that poker.

Blood would have spattered all over her face and neck. Damn Red. Greenwald had probably gone into a bathroom —most likely the one Red had contaminated—and cleaned up.

Greenwald was twisting her hands together, but she

had stopped talking. It felt like she had gone deep into herself.

"So," Rodriguez said a little louder than she had been speaking before, "did you ever touch him?"

"What?" Greenwald lifted her head. "Who? I told you about the butler."

"The naked man," Rodriguez said, choosing *naked* instead of *dead*, so that Greenwald wouldn't focus on the real reason for this interview.

Greenwald's gaze met hers. A small frown creased Greenwald's forehead.

"If I'm understanding you correctly," Rodriguez said, "if you touch someone, you see their death date. Is that right?

"Yes," Greenwald said.

"So did you touch him? Did you see his?" Rodriguez had to hold herself back from asking the next question, which was *Did the death dates match?*

Greenwald shuddered. "No. No, of course not," she said. "He was naked, and he was going to hurt me, and if he succeeded in killing me, I didn't want to know he was going to live for another fifty years."

"But you didn't know how he would live, did you?" Rodriguez asked before she could stop herself. "Maybe he would end up in prison."

"Maybe." Greenwald looked down at her hands, and Rodriguez silently cursed herself. She had broken the flow right after it had started again. "I just...I didn't expect it."

Rodriguez waited again, hoping to reclaim that flow, but Greenwald didn't go on.

So finally, Rodriguez said, "Didn't expect what?"

"How determined I was," Greenwald said. "I didn't even think about it. I just defended myself."

Rodriguez nodded. "You grabbed the poker…"

"And he didn't even turn around. I hit him and…" Greenwald looked a little green, her skin going pasty. "He fell forward. It took some yanking to get the poker back, but he didn't fight me."

The back of the man's head looked like he had been hit several times. Greenwald had clearly hit him repeatedly. It must have been some kind of frenzy.

Usually people who fell into one, however, didn't remember the details of it. Or just one detail.

And it seemed like the detail that Greenwald remembered was getting the poker stuck in the man's skull.

Rodriguez hoped that Piña was getting all of this. Because they had the necessary confession. It would be up to the district attorney to figure out how to use it.

The crazy stuff could cause a problem. But that wasn't Rodriguez's problem.

"I didn't know what to do," Greenwald said, and Rodriguez made herself focus on the words right now, not on the upcoming case. "I mean, I suppose I could have not called you at all."

It took a brief second for Rodriguez to catch up. Greenwald wasn't talking about what to do after she had destroyed a man's skull with a poker. She was talking about calling 911.

"I mean," Greenwald said, "I actually had to think about it for a minute. Since today is my death day and I wasn't planning to leave the villa, I would die here somehow, and then some poor maid or something would have found both of us tomorrow."

Rodriguez opened her mouth to say, *That would have happened anyway if you had died here*, but stopped herself just in time. Understand the crazy; don't live in the crazy.

"And then I realized that—well, I mean, they probably find dead people all the time. Heart attacks in their sleep or drowning in the pool." Greenwald's eyes opened wide. "And, no, I haven't gone near the pool. Right now, everything is a potential hazard. I mean, what if I slipped on the concrete, hit my head, and fell in?"

Rodriguez didn't move. The flow was back. She wasn't even sure if Greenwald was really talking to Rodriguez anymore or was simply just talking.

"But, you know," Greenwald said, slipping her hands apart and gesturing with one of them. "All that blood. I didn't think some poor person just trying to make a living should see that."

Rodriguez hadn't expected that tiny bit of compassion. It was odd, but then this whole case was odd.

"So I called you people," Greenwald said. "But I didn't expect an army to come in here and deal with it. I figured you could help me and then get me somewhere safe."

"We would like to," Rodriguez said.

"I'm not even sure what that would be," Greenwald said. Then she shifted slightly in her chair and looked at the door. "Do you think that the butler is done yet? We can ask him."

"I'm sure someone will let us know when he is," Rodriguez said, even though that wasn't what would happen at all. "May I ask you one other question?"

Greenwald turned her head slightly. Those colorless eyes moved and met Rodriguez's. There was awareness in those eyes, but they seemed detached, distant.

Rodriguez couldn't tell if that was shock or if that was how Greenwald always was.

"Did you know the man who came into this room?" Rodriguez asked.

"No!" Greenwald said. "No, of course not. I didn't want anyone here, and then this man comes in and takes off his clothes, and heads for the bedroom. And I knew, I *knew* that he was wanted to surprise me and he would attack."

Then she took a deep breath and stopped herself.

"I'm just trying to figure out how he got in here," Rodriguez said. "Maybe someone sent him...?"

"Like what? A flower delivery?" Greenwald asked. "Who would do that?"

There was an edge to her now, as if she was beginning to realize she had talked too much.

Or had she? Was this all a ploy to protect herself by

trying to be crazy enough that the courts would let her plead by reason of insanity?

That wasn't Rodriguez's job to figure out. Right now, she needed to move this all forward.

"You tell me," she said, keeping her voice modulated. But she wasn't going to baby Greenwald any longer.

"What do you mean?" Greenwald asked.

Rodriguez stopped leaning forward. She sat up straight and allowed her expression to grow harder.

"It's nearly impossible to get into this room without your permission," Rodriguez said. "And to get naked in this room? I think that would need your permission as well. What did he really do?"

"I *told* you!" Greenwald clasped her hands over her mouth, then let them down. The agitated movements started again. "I didn't let him in. He *got* in."

"How?" Rodriguez asked.

"I don't know!" Greenwald folded her hands in front of her face, then tapped her thumbs against her chin. *"I don't!* I thought this place was secure. That's why I came here, so no one could bother me, but then, it seemed *everyone* could bother me. There's the stupid butler that they wouldn't let me get rid of and I asked for no maid service, but they said everything needs to be refreshed every day, and I finally got them to cancel that, and then…and then…and then…"

She was stammering, deeply upset. Rodriguez wanted to lean back in case Greenwald decided to become violent again, but it didn't look like she was going to.

"...and then, this *person* came in, because they have something called turn-down service, and they marched right into my bedroom and grabbed my bed and I told them to leave or I would call security and the butler, he had to settle everyone down."

"When was that?" Rodriguez asked, trying to figure out how someone doing turn-down service would end up naked.

"Last night! Last night, when I figured out I wasn't going to be secure here after all, and it was so unpleasant. I didn't pay for that. I paid for privacy, but I guess, I was going to have to pay more. That's what last night's butler said, that some people pay more to keep the staff out of the rooms."

A shake-down. Rodriguez bet the hotel wasn't going to like that.

"And that butler was working today?" she asked.

"No!" Greenwald was yelling now. Some of the crime scene analysts had stopped when the yelling started, because they clearly wanted to see what was going on, but they were professionals. They went right back to work.

However, some of the remaining officers made their way silently into this part of the villa.

"I called the desk and asked for a manager. I told them I needed someone else up here because that butler tried to extort me."

"And that was when the new butler showed up?" Rodriguez asked.

"A new butler. I had to share with the room next door, and I didn't care. I said that butler could go there for all I cared, and then I stayed in the room." Greenwald's voice shook. A tear ran down her face. "I wanted privacy. I wanted *safety*. I figured avoiding people was the only way I was going to avoid dying."

There were a million ways to die without the help of other people. Slipping in the shower. Drowning in the bathtub or the pool. Having a heart attack or a stroke, with no one around to call for help. Severe food poisoning or a serious allergic reaction. Tons of ways to die and they all ran through Rodriguez's head, before she caught herself.

"So you think the butler, today's butler, let him in," Rodriguez said.

"How else could he have gotten in? I didn't do it. And he had a key."

Rodriguez wasn't sure she had heard that before. She almost asked about it but stopped herself instead.

"Tell me what you saw when he let himself into the room," she said.

"Why?" Greenwald asked.

"Because this is suspicious," Rodriguez said, hoping that would be enough to placate Greenwald into continuing to talk.

One of the officers crossed his arms. Another leaned against the wall, his body so tense that it looked like he was going to launch himself forward if something went seriously wrong.

"You think they did something?" Greenwald asked. "You think someone is out to get me?"

"I'm new to this," Rodriguez said. "If you give me more information, I'll be able to answer your questions."

Maybe just not in the way you want me to, she did not add.

Greenwald took a deep breath. Maybe it was meant to be steadying, but it was shaky.

"I was in the kitchenette, making myself a sandwich when I heard the door open," she said. "I thought maybe it was another hotel employee violating my space, so I peered out the door. I wanted to see what, exactly, was going on."

Rodriguez nodded, knowing the importance of keeping her talking.

"This guy walked in like he owned the place. He was whistling. Whistling!" Greenwald's voice was getting progressively louder.

Rodriguez almost asked if she had called out to him, but Greenwald had moved into another long story, and in this discussion, Rodriguez had learned that interrupting Greenwald stopped her from saying something important.

"He walked right into the bathroom, and I didn't know what to do!" Greenwald said. "I mean, what employee goes into a bathroom? He didn't have a cart or anything. And he didn't introduce himself either, you know, like they do, shouting 'Housekeeping' or whatever."

Rodriguez folded her hands together and concentrated on them, so she would not ask any questions until Greenwald slowed down.

"I thought maybe he had to use the bathroom. He stopped whistling and I thought maybe there'd be the sound of peeing or something, but I didn't hear anything. Then there were two thuds. Loud ones, and I got even more scared."

She was almost hyperventilating now, and she was on the edge of the chair, almost like she needed to stand up, but wasn't going to, not yet.

A couple of the officers had moved closer.

"So, I figured I had a moment. I went into the fireplace room and grabbed the poker. I figured I could fend him off with that, and maybe scream or something, and maybe the stupid butler would hear that and come in."

Not likely. Those butlers had probably heard lots of untoward things through the door...if the door wasn't soundproofed, which Rodriguez suspected it was.

"I moved against the wall—" Greenwald waved a hand at one of the walls near the dining area. "—just as he came out of the bathroom, and he was naked. Like it meant nothing. Naked. And that's when I knew what he was going to do. He was going to wait for me in the bedroom and rape me and then he was going to kill me. I don't know why me, maybe because of this room, but he was going to do it and I couldn't let it happen, so I ran after him and I hit him."

She stopped suddenly as if she heard herself. But she wasn't looking at anyone.

"I hit him," she said.

"Why didn't you just leave?" Rodriguez asked.

"Because the butler had to let him in. They were probably in on it. Or maybe someone else with a key, like last night's butler. You don't understand how scary it was. You don't understand. He was going to kill me."

Rodriguez did understand. She understood that Greenwald was paranoid and hadn't been thinking clearly. She had thought there was no other option but to attack the man she thought was going to attack her.

Which was, in Rodriguez's experience, the best way to get killed.

But she didn't say that.

Instead, she stood up. She signaled one of the officers standing behind Greenwald. He grabbed his handcuffs and walked over, moving quietly.

"Sabrina Greenwald," Rodriguez said, "you're under arrest."

Legally, she no longer had to recite a Miranda warning, but she did anyway, just to protect her investigation. Greenwald was looking at her, and then at the officer, and she tried to twist away.

"You can't take me out of here," she said. "I could die in your jail. I could be attacked. How do you know he won't hurt me? Or someone might shoot us? God, I thought you understood—"

"Take her out of here," Rodriguez said to the officer.

He put a hand on Greenwald's shoulder, and she screamed, pivoting around and trying to bite him. Another officer came over, and together, they hauled her out of the room.

She yelled all the way to the door and beyond. There were banging noises, as she probably ran into a wall or hit something.

Then the noises grew silent. Rodriguez didn't know if that was because the elevator had arrived to take Greenwald away or if the officers ordered her to be quiet.

Piña took her phone out of her pocket and shut off the recording.

"That was weird," she said.

Rodriguez did not offer judgment. Piña still wore a body camera, although it probably wasn't on. Still, Rodriguez didn't want to say anything that would jeopardize this case.

She'd learned that from long, hard experience.

She looked at the chair where Greenwald had been sitting, and sure enough, there were some smears that were probably blood.

Rodriguez called a crime scene analyst over, and pointed to the chair. "Make sure you get that."

Rodriguez wanted to make sure it was right, even though she had a feeling that they wouldn't be hurting for evidence in this case.

She made her way around the little chair grouping and stopped at the bathroom door. There were two analysts inside.

The room no longer smelled of vomit, but faintly of

chemicals. Men's clothes were piled near the standalone tub, along with two shoes that were resting haphazardly on their sides.

The man taking them off was probably the two thuds that Greenwald had heard.

What kind of person would walk, whistling, into a hotel room, peel off his clothes and his shoes, and then walk into the bedroom?

None of that made sense if he was going to attack someone.

Rodriguez moved away from the bathroom and headed to the bedroom.

There were two more analysts here, as well as one who was working on Red. The idiot was probably going to get into a lot of trouble. Fortunately for him and the department, this case probably wouldn't ever get to a trial. Rodriguez had more than enough evidence to convince even the most shark-like defense attorney to take a plea deal.

"Got a picture of the guy's face yet?" Rodriguez asked Karni Feeney, the head analyst. She was a heavyset woman with tired eyes.

"Yeah," Feeney said. "You want it?"

"I do," Rodriguez said. "Send it to me."

Normally, she would ask for an airdrop, but she wanted something that would stand up to chain-of-custody rules.

Feeney moved to one side, and worked the screen of

her phone with her thumb. While she did that, Rodriguez looked at the room.

There was no weapon other than the fireplace poker. Nothing that could even be used as a weapon, like rope or string or nylon to cover the face.

According to Greenwald's own statement, she hit the man as soon as she could catch up to him.

"Was there anything underneath the body?" Rodriguez asked. "A knife, a gun, some kind of weapon?"

"No," one of the other analysts said. "And his hands are empty."

"What about under the bed?" Rodriguez asked. "Anything that could be used as a weapon?"

"No," the other analyst said. "There's nothing here. The guy came in buck naked, and if he was carrying anything, we didn't find it."

That actually matched with Greenwald's story. She hadn't seen anything either. She just thought that the guy was going to assault her before he killed her.

"Any idea who he is?" Rodriguez asked.

"I think there's a wallet in the bathroom," one of the analysts said. "You'll have to ask there."

Rodriguez nodded and was about to head back when Feeney said, "I sent you the picture."

"Thank you," Rodriguez said.

She double-checked her email photo, and sure enough, the photograph was there. She clutched the phone, planning to head out the door, but she peered into the bathroom again.

"Find a wallet?" she asked.

"We did," said one of the analysts, "but we haven't confirmed the identity yet. You want it?"

She had decided, after that confession, she was going to do the rest of this by the book. Too many detectives figured a confession was more than enough, only to have it thrown out on some weird-ass technical reason.

She made her way to the main door. Some of the officers were gone now that Greenwald had left, and what few remained looked idle. She might have to assign them tasks if Weaver didn't get around to it.

But right now, Rodriguez was focused. She pushed open the door only to find the butler's post empty.

She bit back an exclamation of annoyance. He was the man she wanted to see.

Then she did see him, standing near that god-awful floral arrangement, hands clasped in front of him. An officer stood beside him, apparently awaiting instructions.

She gave the officer instructions. She told him to record this next conversation.

"You're the butler that was on duty today?" Rodriguez asked, stopping in front of that stinky arrangement. Her nose tickled again.

"Yes, ma'am." The butler's voice was soft. He had his head down slightly, revealing the beginnings of a bald spot near his crown.

"I understand you were not at your desk all day like you were supposed to be," she said.

"I followed the rules, ma'am," he said, his cheeks flushing. "We get a ten-minute break every hour."

"And the desk is empty then?"

"No, ma'am," he said. "Another butler mans the desk. Usually one in training."

"And what happens when a butler has a personal bathroom emergency that can't wait?" she asked.

His flush got deeper. "I send for the back-up. We all do. The desk isn't unmanned for more than a minute or two, however long it takes the elevator to get here."

"How does someone get into a room without a key?" she asked, deliberately keeping him off-balance.

"Ma'am?"

"Ms. Greenwald said that she didn't let the man in. I'm sure the security footage will back that up. If the other butler didn't let the man in, then the man got in on his own. How does that happen?"

"I don't know, ma'am." The butler sounded heartbroken. His job at this resort was probably finished. Maybe even his career.

She took out her phone, still open to the photo of the deceased.

"Do you recognize this man?" she asked.

All of the color left the butler's face. Clearly, he recognized the deceased.

"That's Davis Jennings," he said. "He's in the villa next door."

Well, not anymore, she almost said.

"Next door?" she asked.

"Yes, ma'am. He rented that one."

"Would his key card work on this lock?" she asked.

"No, ma'am, it shouldn't." But he didn't sound as certain as he needed to.

"It shouldn't, but maybe it did...?" she asked. "How would that be possible?"

His face flushed again. "Mr. Jennings, he's one of our regulars. He has a habit of losing his key card."

She waited, slightly fascinated by the way that the butler's face kept changing color.

"He goes back and forth between villas when he's here. He takes whichever one is open."

"So he's familiar with both of them," she said.

"He's here all the time," the butler said.

She put that aside for a moment. "And he has one of your key cards? The kind that opens all the rooms?"

"Oh, God, no!" The butler sounded horrified. "We would never have given that to him. He would have lost it immediately."

"All right," she said. "Was the key card from a previous visit?"

"No, ma'am. They deactivate on the check-out date. The key cards are just worthless bits of plastic then. We don't even recycle them."

"Then how did he let himself into the room? Was Ms. Greenwald lying about not knowing him?"

"I don't know if she knew him," the butler said, "but they never ever interacted, not in my presence. She was adamant about not wanting anyone near her. And I mean anyone. I can't imagine that she would have talked to him or any other guest."

Rodriguez couldn't imagine it either but she had to ask.

"All right, then," she said. "Be honest. How did he get into the room?"

"He had to have a card," the butler said miserably.

"And how did he get that card?" she asked.

He closed his eyes. This was probably the moment that would get him fired, and he obviously knew it.

He was probably drawing enough strength to stay quiet. If he didn't say another word, Rodriguez would have to work with him and a lawyer. She didn't want to do that.

Then his eyes opened.

"We keep three extra key cards in our desk for the guests," he said. He sounded reluctant to tell her this. "We used to have our own key card maker, but that created too many problems and got one of our butlers fired for misusing it, so we got the extra cards and kept them near the door."

"Show me," she said.

The butler walked to the desk and pulled open a single drawer beneath the slanted top. Inside were mints, some cash, pens, notepads from the hotel, a few buttons, and devices that were small and impossible for Rodriguez to figure out from where she stood.

And then there were the key cards. Two of them.

The butler pulled them out and bowed his head.

"I thought there were supposed to be three," Rodriguez said.

"There were," he said. "There are."

"Would you have given a card to Mr. Jennings?" Rodriguez asked.

"I haven't given anyone a card in weeks," he said.

"Would the other butlers?" she asked.

"Today? No. The secondary butler has to wait for the main butler to return. I'm the only one who can hand out a second key card." He wiped a hand over his face. He clearly knew something.

"Continue," she said.

He shook his head, but it wasn't a *No, I'm not going to tell you* shake. It was an *I can't believe this* shake.

"I know that Mr. Jennings knew where the extra key cards were. If no one was at the desk, he might have helped himself."

If that was the case, security footage would back it up. And all of that would explain Jennings' behavior. He couldn't open the door, thought he had lost his card—or maybe he had lost his card—and grabbed a new one.

Then he went inside what he thought was his room. Greenwald had not personalized the space. Her clothing wasn't lying around. There wasn't even a book on a coffee table or a blanket flung along a couch.

So if he hadn't personalized his either, there was nothing to alert him that he was in the wrong room, especially since he had been in that room many times before.

He walked to the bathroom (and that explained the whistling) to maybe take a shower or use the jacuzzi tub and disrobed. Then he went into the bedroom—for what? A robe, maybe? A nap before the shower? Maybe just to change clothes?

And that was when Greenwald assaulted him.

Rodriguez sighed. A simple mistake. One that cost a man his life.

Rodriguez nodded at the butler, and then went back to work, knowing she still had some duties ahead of herself.

She needed to inform a family that one of their loved ones had died senselessly.

And then she needed to make the case against his murderer ironclad.

Three hours later, Rodriguez returned to Metro. She had evidence. She had security footage. She had the notepad that Piña had filled out during the interview.

Rodriguez set it all down on her desk in the detective's division of the large glass and chrome building. She had stopped for only a moment, before heading back out to get something to eat.

Weaver caught her in the hallway. He was wearing his civilian clothes, clearly on the way out after his shift.

"You heard, right?" he asked.

She glanced at him. She hadn't really done so until now. He looked white-faced and shaken.

"No, I haven't heard anything," she said.

"Sabrina Greenwald is dead," he said.

"What?" No one had told Rodriguez. Shouldn't someone have told her? "When? How?"

"Freak accident," he said. "At the parking garage at the hotel. No one told you?"

"No," Rodriguez said, feeling something like fury start through her. If Greenwald had died in the parking garage, then she'd been dead for a while now. "What happened?"

"She was freaking out," he said. "She was fighting them, and biting them, and no one could get a good grip on her to put her in the squad."

Rodriguez felt the blood leave her face. She knew what was coming next, because it was procedure.

"They tasered her," she said.

"Yeah," he said.

"And it killed her," she said.

"No," he said. "They weren't holding her tightly enough. She fell and hit her head on the concrete."

Greenwald's voice filled her mind: *I haven't gone near the pool. Right now, everything is a potential hazard. I mean, what if I slipped on the concrete, hit my head, and fell in?*

Rodriguez made herself set the statement aside. You had to approach the crazy, but you couldn't live there.

But this was a hell of a coincidence, wasn't it? Not many people died from being tasered, but some did. And some people died when they hit their head just right.

It was just a coincidence.

It had to be.

A coincidence that would change the disposition of the entire case. She still had to investigate, she still had to report, but now, with the perpetrator dead, it would be mostly informational.

Rodriguez sighed. She had a lot more work to do now.

"All right," she said to Weaver. "I know you're off, but you're going to have to come with me, and help me figure out who to talk with."

"No problem," he said.

And then they looked at each other for a moment. It seemed like he wanted to say more. So did she.

But she wasn't going to.

She wasn't going to think about it at all, no matter what was coming next.

Although, she had to admit privately, knowing she would never tell anyone else, that she was happy about one thing. She was happy that she never touched Greenwald... and Greenwald never told her when her death day would be.

Or Rodriguez would be afraid of it.
Just like Greenwald had been.

BUT WAIT, THERE'S MORE!

Want more masterful mysteries?

Go to wmgbooks.com!

Sign up for the Kristine Kathryn Rusch newsletter, and keep up with the latest news, releases and so much more— even the occasional giveaway.

To sign up go to kriswrites.com

Get the latest news and releases from all of WMG's authors and lines, including Kristine Grayson, Kris Nelscott, *Pulphouse Magazine,* and so much more...

To sign up, **go to wmgbooks.com.**

ABOUT THE AUTHOR
KRISTINE KATHRYN RUSCH

Kristine Kathryn Rusch sold more than 35 million books worldwide. She publishes bestselling science fiction and fantasy, award-winning mysteries, acclaimed mainstream fiction, controversial nonfiction, and the occasional romance.

Her novels made bestseller lists around the world and her short fiction appeared in more than twenty best-of-the-year collections. She won more than twenty-five awards for her fiction, including the Hugo, *Le Prix Imaginales*, the *Asimov's* Readers Choice award, and the *Ellery Queen Mystery Magazine* Readers Choice Award.

To find out more about her work, go to her website, kriswrites.com

facebook.com/kristinekathrynruschwriter
patreon.com/kristinekathrynrusch
bookbub.com/authors/kristine-kathryn-rusch

www.ingramcontent.com/pod-product-compliance
Lightning Source LLC
Chambersburg PA
CBHW030215130726
47898CB00012B/1034